"THE HERB FOR THE SERVICE OF MAN."—
Psalm civ. 14.

"THE BLOOD OF THE PEOPLE SHALL BE ON
THE WATCHMAN'S HEAD, IF HE SOUND NOT
THE TRUMPET."—Ezekiel xxxiii. 4, 5, 6.

THE VACCINE WATCHMAN:

Showing the awful effects of corrupting the
blood with fifty different kinds of disease
through vaccination.

Proving that the practice of corrupting pure blood
with disease, to prevent disease, is an insult
to common sense.

The opinion of eminent physicians is that more
people die through improper medical treatment than from all other causes.

It shows how heavily the public is taxed to support
a useless, sinful, disease-creating practice—
namely, VACCINATION.

It gives a remedy which has never failed to cure
small pox, &c.—Testimonials of wonderful
cures effected.

Names of doctors who failed to cure (if required) from

W. D. STOKES, Medical Botanist,

35, CALVERLEY ROAD, TUNBRIDGE WELLS, KENT.

INDEX TO "VACCINE WATCHMAN."

A SOLEMN WARNING
TO THE PUBLIC.

D EAR READER, by reading the whole of this,
it might be the means of saving your money
and life. Beware of the doctors that profess
to be a blessing to suffering humanity. These lines
can only show the reader a few of the wicked devices
and snares to deceive rich and poor; and show up a
little of the crime and fraud carried on under a cloak
of deception, to make gain. Space will not permit
me to give many names and addresses, or all the
figures from the **statistics**; but I give **sufficient** to
prove my alarming but truthful statements. Were
I to use the names of the following surgeons and
physicians to a false statement it would be a libel,
but thousands of medical men can prove this statement, and the facts stated in a book which I have
written, entitled " Truth *versus* Error: or the Fallacies
of the Medical Faculty Exposed."

It is the opinion of thousands of honest doctors
that tens of thousands of people are murdered in
in England every year, and the constitutions of
millions injured, by poisonous minerals being
used in medicine, and in the adulteration of
food and drinks; and by that unreasonable,
unscientific, useless, filthy, blood-poisoning practice
of vaccination. Who but a mad man or an unscientific, natural fool, would think of taking matter
that had passed through millions of diseased
and filthy people, and putting it into pure blood
to prevent disease? which can only corrupt the blood
with a complication of diseases. It can be proved by
20,000 doctors, and the **statistics**, that vaccination,
either from the animal or human blood, is no preventative from small-pox, but it corrupts the blood
with consumption and about 50 internal and external
diseases.

Read the following, it is only a hint at the villany
carried on, and you will not wonder at John Mason

Good, M.D., F.R.S., saying that the science of medicine is a barbarous jargon, and the effects of our medicines on the human system are in the highest degree uncertain, except, indeed, that they have **destroyed more lives than war, pestilence, and famine combined.** Dr. Frank says that thousands are annually slaughtered in the quiet sick room. Government should, at once, either banish medical men and proscribe their blundering art, or they should adopt some better means to protect the lives of the people than at present prevail, when they look far less after the practice of this dangerous profession and the murders committed in it than after the lowest trades. These are the opinions of two eminent physicians, but I could publish the names of a thousand doctors who are of the same opinion.

Now for a most important question, Vaccination ! which concerns every one. Even those that have no children, and do not believe in vaccination, are heavily taxed to support this arbitrary, useless, disease-creating law. I will now show the value of this beautiful so-called preventative from small-pox, which our English government paid £30,000 **for, nearly 90 years ago.** The cruel unjust monster, Dr. Jenner, introduced this filthy, murderous scheme, to make trade for the doctors, who laboured to get the inventor of this so-called protection against small-pox this £30,000 ; but before he really got the money for this wonderful discovery many doctors proved that this cow-pox vaccination was no preventative against small-pox. But, like the blood-poisoning vaccinator of the present time, this impostor had friends in court, or in parliament, who got him the grant for the money.

Dr. Jenner had only just received the £30,000, when he was obliged to confess to his medical brethren and others that vaccination from the cow **was of no use.** But he said that matter taken from the greasy-heeled horse was a preventative from small-pox. He used it, and served it out to other doctors.

Dr. Collins, and many other physicians, have proved that this horrible, stinking, filthy disease of grease in the horse's heel is always caused by the horse being consumptive. A great many doctors say that the cow-pox, small-pox, the grease, and consumption, is all one kind of disease. This accounts for so much small-pox panic after so much vaccination, and so many dying in consumption.

Dr. Nittinger says, out of 100 small-pox patients before vaccination from five to seven died, but after, from 10 to 20. This might be easily accounted for. The stream of corruption having passed through millions and taken up all kinds of disease, when put into pure blood it must sow the seed for a complication of diseases. This weakens the body, and lowers the vitality, so that when small-pox takes the half-murdered victim, there is not the strength to throw off such a complication of diseases, which is fifty times worse than small-pox alone. This accounts for small-pox being more fatal in the vaccinated than what it is in the unvaccinated, as shown above.

There have been a lot of murderous villains who cared not what they did to make money. They took small-pox matter from their patients, and inoculated the cows, calves, and heifers, and after they had given the animals the small-pox they took the matter from the animal (which was likely to be compounded with syphilis, leprosy, eczema, and other diseases that had passed through millions of filthy people), and put it back into human blood again, and by so doing those wholesale murderers have, at different times, caused fearful outbreaks of small-pox. But those villains professed that after the small-pox matter had passed through the cow that it would prevent small-pox, when put back into human blood, **where they took it from.** To say that it will prevent small-pox is a lie to cover their villany. That which we sow we must reap. The villains did this to keep up their money-making practice of vaccination, which brings in the doctors millions of

pounds every year. Small-pox, when taken in a
natural way by infection cannot be so dangerous as
when inoculated into the body by vaccination, which
is inoculation. Some honest physicians, who were
public vaccinators, have given up the practice **with
disgust**, and are now spending time and money to
make known the **awful effects** of vaccination. Many
found that it caused small-pox, consumption, and
other diseases, which resulted in death.

Dr. Collins writes as follows. A lady had herself
vaccinated, it produced the worst form of small-pox,
which proved fatal. Dr. Collins vaccinated a child;
a few days after, the child was taken with small-pox
and died. This same physician says that there were
eight children vaccinated, and soon after vaccination
small-pox appeared, and on the ninth day of the
disease, with one exception, all died. These are his
own words. "I have met with many similar cases
during certain epidemic outbreaks of the small-pox,
especially when I have inoculated with fresh lymph
from the cow, which, by the way, is obtained by first
passing the small-pox virus through the body of the
animal, and is then said to possess the power of
rendering the human body unsusceptible to small-pox
contagion, but which, in reality, is often the means of
giving the disease it is supposed to prevent."
(Dr. Collins, M.D., M.R.C.S., England.) This is a
murderous practice, philosophically viewed. One,
not only unnatural and disgusting, but an insult to
common sense.—W. D. S.

Many physicians say that the filthy practice of
inoculating cows with small-pox is carried on in
other countries to keep up this money-making
business. It looks very much like it. For in
Germany the vaccinating law is strictly enforced.
The child is vaccinated in infancy, vaccinated at
school age, vaccinated again in case of epidemic or
an outbreak of small-pox, and the males are vaccinated again on joining the army. See, in spite of
this flimsy barricade of double and triple vaccination,
one million of Germans were struck with small-pox

at one outbreak with a most fearful mortality, for 200,000 of those so-called protected people died with small-pox, after being vaccinated three, four, and some five times. In London, the Metropolitan Asylums Board record in their report the admission of 36,000 vaccinated small-pox cases, and these constitute **36,000 failures.** I wonder what will induce the vaccinators to condemn this murderous practice, if these statistics will not do it. Take away the millions of pounds that the public is taxed to pay, and hold the doctors responsible for the ill effects of vaccination, and it would be instantly swept away in disgust.

Dr. Playfair said, in parliament, that another parliamentary screw (he meant a more compulsory law for vaccinating) would sweep small-pox off the earth. How is it that it does not do it in Germany, where all are vaccinated, and re-vaccinated and trebly vaccinated? How can he prove it to be a preventative? seeing that soldiers and sailors, who are all vaccinated and re-vaccinated, die of small-pox. If any anti-vaccinating member were to bring the above, and the following figures, before him, it would prove him to be a man speaking against his own conscience, and, by so doing, he is upholding robbery and murder. On the committee that the government appointed to inquire into the effects of vaccination, they were nearly all interested vaccinators, making a rich harvest by vaccination. What kind of report could they expect? Now hear the words of their leader, who was sent to the government by the interested vaccinators. Dr. Playfair said these words in parliament. We may reasonably assume that those who make gain by the practice are clamorous for its continued enforcement, because they feel it could not maintain itself by the evidence of its efficiency. Dr. Playfair has spoken a few words of truth, for vaccination can never recommend itself; and it is those that are receiving millions of pounds for poisoning the blood that are sending in false reports to deceive the government.

A committee of vaccinators sent in a report to the government with words to this effect: that none need fear injuring the health with vaccination, and there need be no fear of communicating diseases. The statistics on this paper prove them to be bare-faced, wilful liars, upholding a murderous law and a filthy, sinful, disgusting practice for gain; and all these vile, cruel monsters consider themselves gentlemen, and they are treated as such by the public. Dr. Playfair and the committee, Dr. Dilke and others, for gain, shut their eyes against the awful effects of vaccination. They all know that it is only a sham protection, creating disease and killing tens of thousands every year. Because small-pox was not so bad when the committee sat, and just now, those interested vaccinators want to say that vaccination has been the cause of it.

Cholera is not so bad as it used to be, but vaccination has not kept it away. I have shown above how small-pox follows vaccination, and the following figures (which are facts) will show how it causes small-pox and many other diseases. I now ask the vaccinators this question, "how is it that small-pox follows double and triple vaccination? How is it that the death rate for small-pox went up to 20 and 50 per cent, when the population only gained 7 per cent.?" Let the anti-vaccinating Members in Parliament bring those statistics, and make the blood-poisoners prove in a scientific way how a corruption that has passed through millions of filthy people can prevent disease. **Demand an answer,** and the blood-poisoners will be defeated. Notice what follows vaccination. At Blackburn, the Government report for March shows that in 1875 there had been awarded over and above the fees to the Public Vaccinators £185 for successful vaccination. **The above figures do not prove it successful.** Now look at it in the next year, 1876, with three streets blockaded, so great was small-pox raging. They only reaped what they had sown. Is not this sufficient to prove that vaccination is no preventative? Is the Government going to be such dupes to be deceived another 80 years, or do they want the opinion of another interested vaccinating committee ? Are they going to give vaccination a trial for another 80 years, to prove whether it is a preventative, when 90 out of every 100 of the small-pox patients (according to the return from the London Small-pox Hospital) have been vaccinated ? Can any honest, sensible man have any faith in vaccination after reading this page of facts ?

In Manchester, the Public Vaccinator received £367 over his fees for perfect vaccination; and Salford £235 over their fees ; the result was the same, a small-pox panic. Look at Birmingham from 1870 to 1874, receiving £893 over their fees, and it was declared the best vaccinated town in the Kingdom. Yet in the same year, 1874, there were 3763 cases of small-pox, 3367 were vaccinated and re-vaccinated. There were in Birmingham altogether from 1871 to 1874, 7706 cases of small-pox, 6795 had been vaccinated, and there were 1270 deaths. Is this a preventative ?

One of the Members said in the House of Parliament that vaccination had stamped out small-pox in Ireland. Soon after there was a fearful epidemic, and fearful mortality. Out of every 100 deaths, 37 were of children under 5 years of age. On Her Majesty's Ship "Octavia," (where all were vaccinated) and about 99 out of every 100 being re-vaccinated, there were 175 cases, and many deaths, including the First Lieutenant. Sir T. Chambers said in the House of Commons, 1871, that Prussia was the best vaccinated country in Europe, yet in Berlin, three times as many died of small-pox as in London, and in another account, eight times as many.

Now to you that believe in vaccination, do you feel you are safe under its **protection** ? Now for a little more decided proof that vaccination is no good, only to make trade for the doctors. Let Dr. Playfair and Dr. Dilke, and all those blood-poisoners that say vaccination is a preventative, or that it mitigates the disease, look at Germany, the Army and Navy, and Mr. Muller's Orphanage, and a thousand other institutions where all have been doubly and triply vaccinated, small-pox has been worse there than where there has been no vaccination. In Mr. Muller's Orphanage where all were vaccinated and about 95 out of every 100 re-vaccinated, there were 293 cases and 18 deaths.

In the army and the navy, where vaccination is enforced, and every one who enlists has to be vaccinated, and about 95 cases out of every 100 are re-vaccinated, the mortality **amongst these is higher than what it is amongst the civil population.** These figures from the statistics and the above experience of Dr. Collins proves vaccination useless, only to create small-pox and a train of other diseases. I give figures which will prove that small-pox has been five times worse since the Compulsory Vaccination Act was passed than what it was before. Those villians that practice vaccination know this to be true. And this has to be taken into consideration. Before the vaccination law, about one-third part of the people or more carried out that foolish law made by our Royal College of Physicians and the Government to inoculate for small-pox. This foolish murderous law was made, for they thought people would get small-pox easier by inoculation than what they would if taken in a natural way, or by infection ; those unwise generals did not calculate that the inoculated persons would infect others, which they did, and thousands died through inoculation and infection from it. And as those that have had small-pox seldom get it the second time, the Royal College of Surgeons and Physicians laboured under this delusion to think if all people were inoculated for small-pox that there would be no more people to take the disease, and in this unreasonable way they thought to stamp out the disease, forgetting that the millions coming into the world would be diseased by the inoculated victims. The Government nor the physicians in those days (or at the present time) had not the good sense to see that they were taking humours that had passed through millions of diseased and filthy people which would be spreading all kinds of disease, when they made a law to inoculate for small-pox and opened King's College Hospital for the purpose. Common sense ought to show anyone that small-pox could not be so bad now as when they used to give small-pox through inoculation, the interested vaccinators say that vaccination is the cause of it, it is false.

When they were about to repeal the murderous law of inoculation which caused one out of every 14 of the population to die of small-pox, the interested inoculators like the interested vaccinators now were against the law being altered to stop the foolish murderous practice of inoculation. If vaccination were not inoculation in disguise, how could small-pox get worse after they repealed the law of inoculation? The following figures, which are the true statistics, will prove my statement :—

	Deaths.
The first epidemic in 1857-58-59	14,244
Second epidemic, 1863-64-65	20,059
Third epidemic, 1870-71-72	44,840

Increase of population from the first to the second epidemic seven per cent. Increase of small-pox in the same period nearly 50 per cent. Increase of population from the second to the third epidemic 10 per cent. Increase of small-pox in the same period 120 per cent. Deaths from small-pox in the first 10 years after the enforcement of vaccination, 1854 to 1863, 33,515 deaths. In the second 10 years, 1864 to 1873, 70,458. Does not this prove that small-pox increased with vaccination? Yes, and so do the taxes come heavy on the public to support this useless disease-creating practice, which is only another name for inoculation. Prior to the passing of the compulsory vaccination law one small-pox hospital was sufficient for the whole of London, now there are six.

The return of the London small-pox hospitals shows that over 90 per cent. of the patients there have been vaccinated. This ought to be sufficient to convince anyone with reason or common sense that vaccination is useless only to create disease. There are two classes of people who cannot see the truth; first, those who are prejudiced and unbelieving, and will not come to the light to read for themselves; and secondly those interested vaccinators who are making millions of pounds by the vile practice.

I will show some of the ill effects of vaccination and prove the Royal Committee of Enquiry to be liars, deceiving the Government by saying that vaccination would not injure the health nor communicate disease. It appears that 430 deaths and over 2,000 cases of injury are reported by the signatures to the census papers which they allege of their own experience to be due to vaccination. All these witnesses are responsible householders, and there are also 290 deaths on the Registrar-General's report as due to official vaccination. It would be tens of thousands if thousands of those interested vaccinators were not doing the same as the following, writing lies on the death certificate to keep up vaccination which brings in millions of pounds. Now for a doctor's own words. "A death from vaccination occurred not long ago in my practice, and although I had not vaccinated the child, yet in my desire to preserve vaccination from reproach, I omitted all mention of it from my certificate of death. Mr. Henry May, M.R.C.S., Birmingham.—*Medical Review*, 1874. I could get the names of a thousand vaccinating doctors that have done this to keep up that money-making murderous practice of vaccination. I have the names of about 1,000 that have been tortured and died in a dreadful state through vaccination, and the names of tens of thousands that have been murdered by vaccination could be published. I hope those who have the means and love in their heart for suffering humanity will yet publish the awful effects of this murderous law more than what I can show here. Thousands die with internal diseases years after vaccination, and no one knows the cause of their suffering and death. Millions have had their constitution ruined.

If there is one member of Parliament who does not know the awful effects of vaccination he ought to know it, and do his duty to the public, and try to do away with an arbitrary law that permits a lot of unfeeling hearted doctors to commit wholesale robbery and murder by corrupting the pure blood with a complication of diseases for which the public has to pay millions of pounds. There is no business transacted in the House of Commons or Lords, of so much importance as the question of vaccination, for **every householder is taxed to pay vaccinators,** to put poisonous humours into pure blood that have passed through millions of diseased and filthy people, and after poor working men have deprived themselves of the common necessaries of life to pay 20 or 30 fines to keep their children from being tortured to death with vaccination, some have at last been cast into prison, their goods sold, and their wives and children turned out in the street, and thrown on **the parish for support.** This law caused one poor woman to murder herself, body and soul; to put herself as she thought out of a miserable existence. That member of Parliament who will uphold this blood poisoning, sinful, filthy practice ought not to be one of the law-makers.

Fifteen female scholars were syphilised by a vaccination from a child whose skin was perfectly clear.

Dr. Lotz has collected fifty separate cases affecting in all seven hundred and fifty individvals with filthy diseases. All this might arise from one apparently healthy child, or from a cow or calf that has been vaccinated and poisoned from human blood.

In 1882 a committee of fifteen vaccinators met at the Council Chamber, Exeter Hall, and instituted a medical enquiry into some important features of the question. There were seven questions asked. The answers to the third question, viz., What diseases

have you known to be occasioned or intensified by
vaccination which are too important however to be
suppressed ? Two hundred and forty-two medical
witnesses, almost all vaccinators, testified to the
following diseases within their own experience,
caused by vaccination—

Abdominal Phthisis.	Gangrenosa.	Prurigo.
Angeiolencitis.	General Debility.	Pyæmia.
Blindness.	Herpes.	Pyrexia.
Boils.	Impetigo.	Rickets.
Bronchitis.	Inflammation.	Syphilis.
Bullæ.	Intensified Ulcera-	Scald Head.
Cancer.	tion.	Scarlatina.
Cellulitis.	Lichen.	Scrofula.
Convulsions.	Marasmus.	Septicæmia.
Diarrhœa.	Meningitis.	Skin Diseases.
Dyscrasia.	Paralysis.	Struma.
Eczema.	Phagedenic Action.	Tuberculosis.
Erysipelas.	Pityriasis.	Variolsid.
Erythema.	Pneumonia.	

I can prove that there are many other diseases
inoculated into the blood by vaccination. There are
over ten thousand doctors who consider vaccination
useless only to create disease, and they are from
long experience, of the same opinion as myself that
vaccination causes the death of **50,000 persons in
England every year,** and it never saved the life of
one single individual. The first royal committee
named in this pamphlet made it appear to the
Government that vaccination **was harmless,** and a
preventative from small-pox. Doctors are not such
fools as to think that a poisonous humour which has
passed through millions of filthy diseased people
can be harmless, and they are not so mad as to
believe that it can do any good. He who upholds
vaccination in Parliament is pleading for those men
who make millions of pounds by poisoning the
blood. He is like a barrister pleading for a gang
of swindlers, house-breakers, or murderers, to get a
verdict in their favour, what does he care, for a
little money, he would set at liberty on the public
such villains who are not fit to live, but there never
was a highwayman, or housebreaker, or murderer

half so bad as the blood poisoning vaccinators who appear to be such nice pleasant gentlemen.

There were 30,000 American soldiers vaccinated, and **ten thousand** out of the thirty thousand **died** in a dreadful state through vaccination, many others had to have their arms cut off to save their lives, and many had their constitution ruined for life.

No reasonable good man would uphold such a murderous law.

I can defy any of those blood poisoners to prove any statement in this pamphlet to be false. This last dreadful slaughter ought to be enough to open the eyes of the law-makers. Reader, never support or vote for a vaccinator who upholds a murderous law. It is said by many physicians that the German vaccinators as well as the English have vaccinated the cows and calves with small-pox matter.

I can prove from the statistics and my own experience, and many physicians say that those poisoned and corrupted with vaccination infect others who have not been vaccinated. Five vaccinated infants took that fearful and supposed incurable disease of Eczema from a child that had it in the blood. The mother of one of these children took the disease by nursing her child, and the woman was in a most frightful state when she came to me. Thousands of parents are now suffering with external and internal diseases taken from their children. There are diseases which might be taken by the breath in kissing, shake of the hand, or even taking a coin, or wiping on the same towel, &c., &c., and disease is carried from one family to another. I have had to prepare medicine for some **bakers, grocers, butchers,** and **others** whose hands and bodies were in a rotten state ; this is the effect of vaccination. These vaccinating doctors ought to be made to eat the food prepared by these filthy people who are in this rotten state.

Some foolish people say vaccination does not concern them. They don't know how heavily we are taxed, and how likely we are to be poisoned by infection from those diseased by the filthy practice.

A doctor in Tunbridge Wells vaccinated a healthy calf to get matter to vaccinate people **(or make patients)**, but by putting a humour that had passed through millions of diseased and filthy people into that healthy animal he caused the death of the calf, for the animal died some months after in a frightful state, with nearly all the flesh off its bones. The complication of filthy diseases that caused the death of the animal was very likely to cause the death of those that were vaccinated from it. Then a false certificate of death is written to hide their murderous work. Thousands die with internal diseases put into their bodies by vaccination 20 or 30 years after.

I should like to know what becomes of the hundreds or thousands of cows and calves that have been vaccinated with small-pox, and from a current of humour that has passed through millions of diseased and filthy people.

After those animals appear to get well are they given to the dogs? No, most doctors (or I should say blood poisoning man-slayers) have too much love for their dogs to give them unwholesome food to poison them.

It is not only my opinion but that of many others, that after these animals get well to all appearance outwardly, they are **sold for human food,** so the **meat, butter, cheese,** and **milk** are made unwholesome and injurious.

There is not a butcher, doctor, or analyst in the world who can tell what is in matter, flesh or blood: for the parents and child may appear to be healthy but the diseases of the forefathers often break out in the third and fourth generation. Man or beast that may appear healthy outwardly, are inwardly full of disease. There is not a doctor in the world if he vaccinates with animal matter can be sure that he will not cause death, or ruin the constitution.

I, W. D. Stokes, 35, Calverley Road, Tunbridge Wells, will forfeit £500 if any doctor can prove this statement false.

Some doctors, to deceive their victims, tell them

that they have vaccinated their own children and themselves; if there is such a fool in the world I pity him. All doctors know the danger attending vaccination, so to deceive they have simply made a scratch in the arm and caused it to be bad, with a chemical poison. In others they put in a little glycerine, still such are deceiving, and upholding the murderous practice of vaccination.

If there was a law made to hold vaccinators responsible for damage or loss of life there would not be a vaccinator to be found in the world.

Some feeling hearted good people cannot believe that there are such cruel villains in the world. But I ask what crime is there but what some will do for gold, especially when they know that they will not be found out by man and protected by law. It is not only vaccination and adulteration, but poisonous minerals are being used in medicine that slay millions of people. If any doctor in the world could prove these alarming fearful statements to be false I will pay him £500 for his trouble. If vaccination were a preventative and it had saved the lives of millions who have died with small-pox, I am sure even then it would be **20 times a greater curse than a blessing.**

The blood poisoning vaccinator is looked on by all those who have any good judgment or scientific knowledge (to know that a current of corrupt humour that has passed through millions of diseased people can be no preventative for disease), to be an unscientific natural fool, or a robber and a murderer. If a vaccinating doctor is such a fool or a rogue he is not a **fit man to be trusted with peoples lives.** If one is vaccinated from a healthy cow, calf, or child, common sense tells us the child or animal must become unhealthy and corrupted with disease before they could get a poisonous matter from it to vaccinate with.

Any unlearned boy 15 years of age ought to know that a humour passing through millions of diseased people must contain the same kind of diseases. The reason that the death-rate is so high, there is such a complication of diseases through vaccination. The diseases of the brute beast, and millions of filthy people mix together that it baffles the wisest doctor to know what disease his patient is suffering from, and if he does know he has nothing to cure it as he rejects the herbal medicine which God sent to cure disease, and uses poisons and minerals which kill more people than all the diseases put together.

If a doctor is so ignorant to think that a humour that has passed through millions of diseased people can improve pure blood and make it unsusceptible to small-pox or any other disease, I pity the poor man, for his delusion must come from a diseased brain, and such ought not to be trusted with the lives of the people.

The reason that the Government close their eyes and will not see the awful effects of vaccination, is that they labour under the delusion that vaccination is some slight protection from small-pox, but it is the contrary as I have proved elsewhere. If it were really a preventative with its present evils, it would be upholding robbery and murder to support the Compulsory Vaccinating Law, and God will bring them to judgment for it.

How dare a man make a law to murder his fellow creature? the corrupting the blood with diseases in vaccination murders in England alone more than **50,000 people every year.** Who but a cruel monster (that had the spirit of a devil) would cause the flesh to rot from the bones of his fellow-creature, and cause millions of little innocent babes to suffer in an agony of pain with the vile sins of filthy people.

The Almighty God, our wise Creator, has made His work **perfect,** and man cannot improve on it, or make it unsusceptible to disease by vaccination, which is a sin and an insult to our Creator. He has sent a medicine to cure all kinds of disease, only many of the doctors (so-called) are such fools that they do not know their business, if they did they

would think nothing of curing small-pox. I have
never failed in one case to cure it for 30 years past.

The Lord our Maker says that He loves those who
love Him by their life, and to injure His children is
like touching the apple of His eye. Woe unto vile
men that rob and murder millions. Woe unto those
that make and uphold such a cruel murderous law
as vaccination. The law is a disgrace to the Members
of Parliament and doctors that support the blood
poisoning practice. I believe that 99 out of every
100 cases of small-pox might be cured; in fact I do
not see why all should not be cured if treated with
harmless herb medicine. I will engage to treat any
case of the worst sort of confluent small-pox; no
cure, no pay, or give advice free to anyone. But
that the public might have a remedy at hand, I will
give them a receipt or a remedy that would have
cured more than three-parts of the people that have
died with small-pox.

When taken ill, or as soon as they know what
they are suffering from, keep out of the cold or
draught, and drink freely of a herb tea made as
follows :—

Take one ounce and a half of the herb yarrow, cut
it up or break it short and make one pint of tea,
strain, sweeten, add a little ginger and cayenne
pepper, drink freely, and keep up a perspiration;
this alone cured one bad case. But in addition to this,
take as much cream of tartar as will stand on a
shilling, and as much Turkey rhubarb as will stand
on a three-penny piece (mixed in a little tepid water)
three times a day; less for a child. And when
small-pox has nearly stopped their breathing, and
they have been very bad inwardly and in the throat,
I have put that right with brewer's yeast and water.
Take half-a-pint of good fresh brewer's yeast and
three of water, mix, gargle the throat often, seven
or eight times a day, spit it out; then take a table-
spoonful of the yeast and water and swallow it three
or four times a day, in addition to the other
remedies; divide the time as near as you can, and

if the yeast or rhubarb should act too freely on the bowels take less of it; omit the cayenne pepper when the herb tea is for a child; give it a teaspoonful of the yeast and water mixed well. I have now made the public a present of a valuable remedy which I never knew to fail for 30 years; but were it to fail I have other valuable remedies. One of my medical assistants took small-pox from one of my patients whilst attending her; I cured him in 24 hours. Mr. Johnson, of Carshalton, came to me on a Saturday evening with all the symptoms of small-pox, a violent cold and inflammation, though there was nothing to be seen on his skin. I gave him the herbal medicine, which drove it out of his system. On the second day after (Monday) he was in a frightful state with confluent small-pox, that is, it was so thick that they ran one into the other, but on the following Monday, which was only the eighth day, he came from Carshalton to my dispensary, feeling himself well enough to go to his office in the City of London; there was a new skin on his face, but not one sore left, or one spot or pit on the skin. I have not failed to cure any kind of disease for 30 years where I have treated the case from the first, and the patient has given the medicine a fair trial. And many hopeless cases after being given up to die by doctors have been cured and the people are now in perfect health. If anyone can disprove the above statements, I, W. D. Stokes, 35, Calverley Road, Tunbridge Wells, will forfeit £100.

The praise be to our Creator who is the giver of all good. He has given us these valuable herbs, which will keep our bodies in a healthy state, if men had the *wisdom* they ought to have, to know how to use them. To the shame of the learned, scientific, medical faculty, that they have not the skill to be able to cure such a simple thing as small-pox. Their remedy or *sham protection*, vaccination, kills a hundred times more than the disease.

A book of great value, full of information, entitled "Truth v. Error," or the fallacies of the faculty exposed, with some valuable recipes, showing how to prevent and how to cure disease, sent post free for one shilling.

DELUSION, FEAR, AND COVETOUSNESS

Are the cause of keeping up the blood poisoning practice of vaccination. Our law-makers are labouring under a delusion to think that corrupting the blood with a complication of disease will prevent disease, or that it is some slight protection to them. This selfish fear causes them to shut their eyes to the awful effects of vaccination which slays millions of people.

This blood-corrupting practice brings me and all the anti-vaccinating doctors (who hate vaccination) gain because it causes so much disease. But the covetousness of the vaccinating doctors who have received millions of pounds for the practice and are still receiving it, causes many of them to swear falsely and forge the statistics; and I have, and can give the names of these doctors who have written lies on the death certificate to keep up this money-making practice.

Why is this horrible cruelty carried out by the above-named gentlemen (so called) **for money.** The Scriptures say that the wicked spirit is allowed to deceive nations of people, because all wilful sinners are in rebellion against God; and this horrible wickedness is only permitted by God for the wicked to fill up the measure of their iniquity. I name this because many have not the spirit of God, or are not wise in spiritual things, and cannot understand why God permits this wickedness to go on. Pray read the following and ask yourself the question, what crimes are there that some would not commit for so many millions of pounds.

PROFITS OF VACCINATION.

As few have any notion of the sum annually spent in this country upon the vaccination of the poor, I

quote the following statement from the annual
reports of the Local Government Board.

PUBLIC VACCINATION.—ENGLAND AND WALES.

	1884.	1885.	1886.
Vaccination fees and expenses ...	£91,938	£94,618	£93,475
Awards or extra to their fees ...	£14,015	£17,687	£18,964
	£105,953	£112,305	£112,439
Numbers vaccinated	504,335	510,719	498,039

So for each one that has their blood poisoned by
vaccination the parish has to pay 4s. 6d., and further
expenses for the illness which vaccination causes.

Few persons are aware of the extent to which the
ratepayers are taxed to support public vaccination;
many indeed believe that the services rendered by
doctors in dispensing the State-enforced prescription
are purely gratuitous. A perusal of the following
statistics will show that this is a delusion.

The Board of Guardians in England and Wales
are the local vaccination authorities of the kingdom.
They have at work under them, for the performance
of vaccinations, more than 3,000 public vaccinators,
and for the remaining part of the business, about
1,400 vaccination officers.

The total cost of public vaccination is made up of
four items:—

I.—Vaccination fees and expenses, paid out of the
poor rate.

II.—Awards, or bonuses, in consideration of the
excellence of the work done by the public
vaccinators; work they have been already paid
for doing under item I. These awards are
paid by an annual grant of Parliament, under
Section 5 of the Vaccination Act of 1867.

III.—Salaries of the itinerant vaccination inspectors
of the Local Government Board.

IV.—The New Government Calf-Lymph Establish-
ment for the Manufacture of Bovine Virus, in
Lamb's Conduit Street.

(Ask the question of the anti-vaccinating Members
of Parliament, What becomes of those calves, not

fit for dogs, as they have been poisoned with the filthy humours from human blood ?)

I.—Vaccination Fees and Expenses arranged in periods of five years.

For the five years ending Lady Day :—

1845	£104,718
1850	120,544
1855	179,175
1860	218,998
1865	257,089
1870	279,571
1875	447,364
1880	437,398
1885	463,380
Total	£2,508,237

Notice how the above fees increase every year, so must our poor rates to support it.

II.—Specimens of the Awards made to Public Vaccinators.

METROPOLITAN.

(The inspections and awards are made every alternate year in the Metropolis.)

NAME OF UNION.	1881.			1883.			1885.		
	£	s.	d.	£	s.	d.	£	s.	d.
Bethnal Green	271	8	0	275	3	0	270	17	0
Camberwell	269	17	0	302	5	0	284	3	0
Chelsea	120	19	0	86	15	0	129	11	0
Hackney	145	6	0	159	3	0	181	10	0
Islington	184	10	0	260	3	0	247	1	3
Lambeth	209	8	0	252	10	0	322	2	0
Marylebone	134	15	0	159	17	0	181	19	0
Mile End	167	7	0	166	19	0	98	11	0
St. Pancras	306	13	0	320	10	0	276	3	0
Wandsworth and Clapham	302	0	0	321	6	0	283	1	0

PROVINCIAL.

NAME OF UNION.	1881.	1882.	1883.	1884.	1885.
	£ s.	£ s.	£ s.	£ s.	£ s.
Birmingham...................... .	235 16	247 11	240 17	240 3	224 12
Brighton	144 12	...	120 13	...	90 6
Keighley	...	0 11	11 7	...	18 1
Liverpool	224 3	211 9	196 7	190 5	175 17
Leicester	...	99 15	...	106 18	...
Manchester	...	140 13	95 15	148 17	119 0
Middlesbrough	...	287 10	...	...	309 10
Prescot	176 1	...	188 19	...	166 12
Salford	331 11	230 8	180 7	183 3	180 16
Sheffield............................	202 7	203 14	183 5	191 10	196 0
Swansea............................	259 10	...	282 15	...	159 15
Toxteth Park	188 13	89 12	107 0	94 12	35 15
West Derby......................	387 14	142 19	223 14	218 5	310 0

These bonuses or awards were first granted in 1868, in which year they amounted to £2,753; in 1872 they had increased to £6,187; in 1878, to £11,994; and in 1885, to £17,687. Notice the increase here.

Total sum awarded in the 18 years, 1868-85, £211,314

The above is extra to the vaccinators' fees.

III.—Salaries and Expenses of the Vaccination Staff of the Local Government Board.

For the year ending March 31st, 1887. From the Civil Service Estimates, ordered by the House of Commons to be printed, February 22nd, 1886.

Medical Officer	£1,200
Assistant Medical Officer	1,000
Two Inspectors at £800 each.........	1,600
One Inspector	700
Six Inspectors £500 to £600 each...	3,567
Assistant Vaccine Inspector	400
Two Vaccinators, £150 each.........	300
Travelling Expenses Amount not clearly defined, but probably over	1,000
Annual Total	£9,767

Ratepayers look at this. The Government appeals

to the above officers for their opinion on vaccination, which is like a publican's opinion on temperance or total abstinence.

IV.—Expenses of the Calf-Lymph Establishment, in Lamb's Conduit Street, Founded 1881.

	1882.	1886.
Director	£400	£400
Assistant Director	150	300
Vaccination Clerk	...	52
Two attendants	100	135
Two servants	...	130
Purchase of lymph, ivory points, tubes, and other apparatus,&c.	900	700
Supply of Calves	300	360
Keep of Calves and incidental expenses	250	800
Cartage of Manure	...	13
Totals	£2,100	£2,890

The public would like to know what becomes of these calves. Are they sold for human food after being vaccinated with humours taken from filthy people.

SUMMARY.

Vaccination Fees and Expenses paid out of the Poor Rates from 1840 to 1885	£2,508,237
Bonuses or Awards paid to the Public Vaccinators from 1868 to 1885	211,314
	£2,719,551

Estimated Annual Cost of Public Vaccination.

Fees and Expenses	£94,000
Bonuses or Awards	17,000
Cost of the National Vaccine Establishment, including the Calf Lymph Station	2,800
Cost of Vaccination Department of the Local Government Board	9,200
	£123,000

The above does not include the enormous fees paid to vaccinators by private families or public schools and colleges.

The millions of pounds which the public has been taxed to pay for corrupting the blood with disease might have been saved, and the lives of one hundred thousand people who have been murdered by vaccination every year if the doctors had used the above-named remedy to cure small-pox. And thousands of others might be cured with harmless herbs of all other kind of disease.

But just as many despise God's law, so they despise the herbs that would give health to our bodies. The vile practice of corrupting the blood by vaccination will never be done away with whilst the Government is led *by the vaccinators* who are making *millions of money* by the practice, or whilst the ruling powers believe vaccination to be the slightest protection against small-pox. When the anti-vaccinating societies will agree together and get a list of people who have had their constitutions injured, and a list of those who have died from the ill-effects of vaccination, and a list of the doctors who caused the death of 100,000 people, old and young, and a list of their lying death certificates that have been written to keep up the *vile money-making practice*, and a list of 15,000 or 20,000 doctors who are against vaccination; these lists will then prove vaccination to be wholesale robbery and murder, and the statistics would show that each epidemic, after the Compulsory Vaccination Act was passed got more severe, and the death-rate and heavy taxation to support the practice increased four-fold. Lists like these, with a few questions put to the vaccinators would overthrow the useless, money-making, murderous practice. Let the anti-vaccinating Members of Parliament bring the vaccinating doctors (who have written false certificates of death) to the law, such doctors ought to **have their diplomas taken away,** and be **held responsible for the damage they have done.** Question 1st.

How can a righteous Government allow doctors to give false certificates and not punish them? 2nd. How can anti-vaccinators support those Members of Parliament who are in favour of compulsory vaccination, seeing that hundreds of thousands are murdered by it? 3rd. **By what authority** does the Government keep up a law to murder millions of people? 4th. What man in his right mind with common sense can think that there is such a thing as pure lymph, or that anyone can be vaccinated from a healthy animal or child, when the doctors have to put corruption (which has passed through millions of diseased people) into pure blood **before they can take it out?** 5th. Can any vaccinating doctor prove in a scientific way how poisonous matter taken from a cow or calf, or from a current of corruption which has passed through millions of diseased and filthy people in vaccinating one from another can improve pure blood and make it unsusceptible to disease? 6th. Can any doctor prove that vaccination does not inoculate internal and external diseases which might cause death many years after? 7th. Can any doctor prove that a great number of cows and calves have not been vaccinated with a current of corruption which has passed through millions of diseased and filthy people? 8th. Can any doctor prove that this humanised lymph (as the doctors call it, after it has been taken from a human being, and passed through the cow or calf, and put back again into pure human blood), does not contain the same diseases that have destroyed thousands of brute beasts, and a train of disease taken from the current of corruption that has passed through millions of diseased and filthy people? Or that it does not cause a **complication of diseases that are incurable?** Or that it does not cause the death of 50,000 people in England every year? Can any doctor prove in a scientific way that vaccination **ever saved one life?** I can get the names and addresses of 20,000 people who have died from the ill-effects of that blood poisoning, murderous practice of vaccination. I can get the names of 10,000 doctors who have no faith in vaccination as a preventative, or to mitigate small-pox, and who say that it is of no use, but to create disease. For this sham protection against small-pox the public are heavily taxed to pay millions of pounds to the blood poisoning vaccinators. Many of them care not what they do to make money.

Many who are against compulsory vaccination are against a **prohibitory law** being made to **stop vaccination.** If a prohibitory law is not made thousands of these blood poisoners will persuade the people that vaccination is good (to make money) and so murder thousands of people. It is right to make a law that will protect the people from impostors.

As the vaccinating doctors often frighten parents into having their children vaccinated, after a certain age, I now give what the Act of Parliament states: "That no parent can be compelled to have his child vaccinated before the age of three months, or after the age of 15 months." Magistrates—when an order to vaccinate is applied for—may grant the order if they think fit, but are under no obligation to do so.

The murderous, filthy practice of corrupting the blood by vaccination might be made harmless, if any one would adopt the following plan. To suck out what the filthy monsters put into the wound in the arm as soon as possible after, and then put on a bread poultice made with milk and water, or, what would be better, a bread poultice made with a strong tea of wood sage. I have a delicate stomach myself, soon turned at any filthiness, but to save life I would not mind doing what I advise my fellow man to do ; only wash out the mouth well with water, or the wood sage tea if you have it. Some have adopted the plan I have laid down, and some have carried a poultice in their pocket, to apply directly after the filthy operation.

The Anti-Vaccinating Society protects children from the man slayers, or blood poisoners, for 5s. a year. Apply, 77, Atlantic Road, Brixton, S.W.

I will now give a few Testimonials concerning Cures effected by the use of harmless herbs, and show the awful effects of poisoning the blood by Vaccination.

Cure of a dreadful disease caused through Vaccination.—

I cured the son of Mr. Whittle, Lyham Road, Brixton, London ; the boy was suffering from a dreadful disease caused by vaccination. He had been suffering fourteen years ; the complaint settled principally in his head, and caused a poisonous matter to run from his ears, resulting in a mass of sores down the sides of his face and on the ears. The nose was very much disfigured. He also had a large tumour on his side, which the doctors painted with iodine ; they tortured the lad in different ways, but could not cure him. I cured this lad in three months— he now enjoys good health, and has had no relapse for over seven years.

Who was the Quack Doctor in this case?

Some children who have been brought to me in a dreadful state, suffering with frightful skin disease and with such a complication of internal and external complaints taken from the brute beast and filthy people through vaccination, that no man on earth could cure— though many have been cured with harmless herbs, after doctors gave them up to die.

A Cancer Cured.—

One of the legal qualified surgeons, Doctress Miss Firth, brought a child to me with a cancer in the knee, which neither she nor other doctors could cure. I was able to cure the child in three months. Mr. Juler's child also had a very painful swelling in the knee, and the leg was swollen as large as a man's leg. The child was first treated by a chemist, who said it was a cold in the muscles of the knee ; he failed to do it any good. It was next treated by Dr. Green, Peckham Road, who first said it was a sprain, and next that it was an abscess : at last he could do no more for the child, as he found it was a cancer. The child was next taken to Dr. Henry, Southwark Park Road, but he had no hope of its recovery. Dr. Wiggings, of Southwark Park Road, Bermondsey, could do nothing for the child. I cured this child's knee in six days ; I charged 3/9 for medicine and embrocation, which effected a perfect cure.

Marvellous Cure of Diseased Hip.—

Miss Jones, eleven years of age, lay in the Hospital a long time with a diseased hip ; the doctors had operated on it and taken out pieces of decayed bone, but the child's sufferings had been so great that she would not stay there. Her parents were told when they took her away from the Hospital that very likely she would die before they could get her home ; however, this was not the case. When I visited this case I took a doctor with me, who said I could do the child no good, and advised me not to torture her but to let her die. We found the poor sufferer lying down, with a large hole in the hip, from which there was a great discharge, and the doctors in the hospital had bound a wide tape or bandage round the leg from the foot to the hip, which stopped the circulation of the blood, it was so tight, and this useless mad trick caused the child great pain. With my wonderful purifying herbal medicine and harmless herb poultices (which cause no pain) I so far cured this hopeless case that in ten days the girl could stand, and was soon able to walk for two hours consecutively.

Who was the Quack Doctor in this case?

Another frightful case of Blood Poisoning.—

Miss Childs, aged 14, residing at 57, Kimberley Road, Evelina Road, Nunhead, Peckham, London, S.E. She had been treated at Guy's Hospital over twelve months for a frightful wound or a hole in her neck large enough to put in an egg ; at the back of her tongue there was a large hole caused by a cancerous ulcer, and another hard swelling with all the appearance of an ulcer forming on the tongue. The doctors wanted to operate on the tongue or cut it out, but to do so they said they must take out some of her teeth. Mr. Childs would not have his daughter tortured any more. She came to me, and I cured her in three months.

Who was the Quack Doctor in this case?

An Injured Spine and a large Wound in the Back Cured.—

Mrs. Rees' daughter, 95, Church Street, Camberwell, London, S.E., was treated by Dr. Edmonds, Southampton Street, Camberwell, for a diseased spine ; he operated on the child, but to no good effect, and he had no hope of the child's recovery. When he left this hopeless case, the child had a frightful wound in the back, and she was doubled up, with her face almost touching her knees. My harmless, painless, herbal remedies effected a perfect cure; she is now a straight, healthy young woman.

Who was the Quack Doctor in this case?

A Wonderful Cure of three dangerous diseases at once—*Diabetes (which is considered incurable), Diphtheria, and Scarlet Fever.*—

This case was the daughter of Mrs. Ritchin, Southwark Bridge Road, London. She was restored to health in a few weeks, with the herbs which our Creator sent for the use of man. I cured a boy of the same family of small pox in a week; another daughter of diphtheria; and another daughter of a bad toe that the doctors wanted to cut off, for it was considered too bad to cure.

Who were the Quack Doctors in these cases?

Frightful Skin Diseases Cured.—

Children who have been swollen and blind with a frightful eruption on the face, which is often caused by vaccination, have been cured, after doctors have failed in their attempts.

Cure of a Cataract in Six Days.—

The daughter of Mr. Thatcher, 11, Mount Pleasant, Merton Road, Wandsworth, was effectually cured in six days, without any pain or operation. She was so blind in one eye that she could not see a man's hand nine inches from her face, or a man if he was one yard from her. At the same time, the girl was suffering with liver disease and debility, so she was too weak for the doctors to operate on. She had been at the various ophthalmic hospitals for over six months, and derived no benefit; she was in the Ophthalmic Hospital, Moorfields, London, and at the Royal Westminster Ophthalmic Hospital, King William Street, Charing Cross, under Dr. Rouse, but found no benefit. The doctors said it would be six months longer before they could put the child under an operation, for her health was so very precarious that an operation might cause her death. With three weeks of herbal treatment the child was restored to health with good eyesight, and able to read the smallest print. I will forfeit £100 if I cannot prove this, or if any one can prove any of these testimonials to be false.

Again I ask,

Who was the Quack Doctor in this case?

The hearing and the speech have been restored, after being lost through disease, and reason given to insane people. A bad case of neuralgia was cured with one bottle of my medicine, after taking medicine from the physician daily for twelve months.

Who was the Quack Doctor in this case ?

Millions of people lose their teeth and have their constitutions ruined, and are great sufferers with neuralgia and liver disease, through taking the deadly poisonous tincture of iron, steel, and mercury, which the doctors drench old and young with ; for there is mercury in the teething powders, worm powders, and gray powders (which are only composed of quicksilver and chalk). Antibilious pills, liver pills, compound rhubarb pills, and nearly all their aperient medicines contain mercury ; and for cough, diarrhœa, and internal pains, they use chlorodyne (a deadly poison, which has caused the death of many), and opium, which deadens pain, causes sleep, so this is used in the murderous stuff called " soothing syrup." These are the quacks that murder millions of people.

Cure of Bad Legs.—

A gentleman had fearfully bad legs for 25 years. The doctor wanted to cut off one leg ; but after a few weeks herbal treatment he was able to walk miles, and work in his garden, but previously to his receiving my treatment he was confined to his house for eight years, not being able to walk out.

A gentleman lying in Guy's Hospital, London, with a frightfully bad leg, which the doctors wanted to cut off, heard of me, and was taken out of the hospital; I treated him and cured him. The names of others cured, with the names of the doctors (so-called) who failed to do any good, but who wanted to cut off legs and arms, could be given.

Many have been robbed of a fortune and tortured by their doctors for many years, and brought to poverty by their medical ignorance or dishonesty, and they still treat these impostors or quacks with respect, and would not have anybody know that their doctors had failed to cure them, but often led them to believe that they had done so ; and rob me or some other herbalist of the credit that was due to us. And many whom I have cured have no love in their hearts for their fellow-creatures, to tell them where they might be cured ; such are not in favour with

God—they are guilty of the sin of omission, omitting to do their duty.

Cure of Lock-jaw, Rheumatic Fever, and Inflammation on Kidneys, Liver, and Lungs.

Mrs. Mitchell, 84, Greenwich Road, Deptford, near London, had been lying fourteen weeks in great pain with rheumatic fever, and could not bear any one to touch her. She was paralysed so that she could not move hand or foot for over three months. She had been treated by Dr. Brookhouse, High Street, Deptford, and Dr. Kirby, in the same street. She could not bear to be moved, and for over three months was not able to feed herself, and for several weeks only able to drink a little beef tea and lemon water. She had lost the use of her limbs for over three months, and not only had those fearful pains in her limbs, but in her right side through inflammation of the liver and fearful pains in the lungs (which were loaded with phlegm), and very bad constipation. She had been jaw-locked three days before I commenced to treat her, and through the bad state of her liver and heart, and the violence of the disease, she was turning very dark in the face, and no one had any hope of her recovery, for it was thought impossible. I prepared herbal medicine for her, *without seeing her*, and told her husband that she would get up in nine days : she got up and came downstairs the ninth day, as I said. I believe the doctor was kept on until she came downstairs, when he was told that his medicine had not been taken since I commenced to treat the case. If those doctors could not cure the woman when she was first taken, or before she was jaw-locked, and turning black in the face, and almost a skeleton, what chance had they of curing when I took her in hand? This great sufferer has enjoyed good health ever since — over four years ago.

Who were the Quacks?

If a doctor has not the wisdom and knowledge to effect cures as I have done, his diploma ought to be taken from him and given to the man who can cure. Valuable information, as a present to the world. Rheumatic fever generally comes on through a cold, and the whole system gets full of inflammation, as it was in Mrs. Mitchell's case. Others might be cured at first with a handful of the herb yarrow ; make a tea with the herb, strain, and sweeten with treacle or brown sugar, add as much ginger and cayenne pepper as will stand on a shilling, drink a cupful or half-a-pint hot in bed, promote perspiration with a few extra blankets and a bottle of hot water to the feet, promote the perspiration all you can, the more the better, and let the patient remain so for one or two hours and then gradually cool down. If the inflammation is on the lungs a hot poultice should be applied, made with crushed linseed four parts, mustard one part. I have never known this treatment fail for 30 years. This treatment at first would cure a lot of other diseases. Heat is life, cold is death. I keep packets of herbs with the right quantities of ginger and cayenne pepper all ready, with the direction how to use it, post free for 9d. The above treatment at first would save the lives of one hundred thousand people that die in England every year. Of course, after patients have been bad for two or three days or more, they would require additional treatment. I am sure that I could have cured this dreadful case of rheumatic fever (Mrs. Mitchell) in four or five days at first when the quack doctors took her case in hand.

I cured a bad case of Rheumatic Fever

In Mr. Sansbury, two doors from the Board Schools, Southampton Street, Camberwell, London, S.E., in thirty hours.

And another bad case of Rheumatic Fever

In Mr. J. Craddock, 105, Camden Grove North, Peckham. He was lying in bed with a burning fever, for his flesh felt quite hot, though in himself he felt very cold ; he was in great pain, unable to move hand or foot, at times delirious. I cured him in four days, and he said that he felt well and free from pain.

A baby cured of Hereditary Consumption,

Having taken it from its mother. The child up to six months of age was like a skeleton, and both lungs in a bad state, and no doctor had any hope of her recovery. I effectually cured this child with two small bottles of medicine, she became the picture of health and strength six months afterwards. This was the daughter of the above-named Mr. Sansbury.

A case of Chronic Rheumatics Cured.—

Mr. Wood was treated in Guy's Hospital for twelve

months and received no benefit. I cured this and many other cases that have been brought to me.

Cure of Liver Disease and Consumption.—

Mr. Mannock, 25, Southampton Street, Camberwell. This was a very bad case of liver disease and consumption ; he laid three months on his back, too ill to turn or to be turned on either side ; he was not able to feed himself, or put a spoon to his mouth, nor able to wipe the perspiration from his face ; to use his own words, " When a fly pitched on my face I had not strength in my arms to thrust it off." Through the diseased liver his right side was much swollen and very painful, causing continual diarrhœa. He was taking medicine at this time from Dr. Parrott (who attended him for some time), he was afterwards treated by Dr. Chabot and Dr. Hague for some time without receiving any benefit. His lungs were diseased from top to bottom, back and front, there were nothing but unhealthy sounds caused by the ulcerated state of his lungs, causing him to spit away a quantity of putrefied phlegm every day. He had very little flesh on his bones, and through laying so many months had frightful sores on his body. I treated this complicated case (that no mortal man could have had any hope of curing) with harmless herbs, and in a few months restored him to health, so far that he went into Mr. Gibbs' corn dealer's shop, opposite his own house and took up a half-hundredweight in each hand, and was strong enough to carry them 200 yards.

Who were the Quack Doctors in these cases ?

Another bad case of Consumption.—

Mr. Wood, Neate Street, Camberwell, age 36, was ill five years, and an in-patient twice at Victoria Park Hospital. The whole time (seven months) the doctors said he was suffering from bronchitis and consumption. He was thirteen weeks in Brompton Hospital ; the doctors there said it was liver disease and congestion of the lungs. He was twelve weeks in St. Thomas's Hospital ; here the doctors said he was in the second stage of consumption. In the St. Andrew's Hospital, Clewer, near Windsor, for fifteen weeks ; there he was told he was in the second stage of consumption. He was also in Lambeth Infirmary, where he received very bad treatment. The doctor in attendance at St. Thomas's was Dr. Thorowgood, and the two Physicians at Brompton Hospital were Drs. Bristow and Richards. Mr. Wood also was treated by private doctors after being all this time in Hospitals, namely, Dr. Walker, 57, Harley Street, Cavendish Square (Head Physician at the Golden Square Chest Hospital); this doctor's fee was one guinea each time, and he told the poor sufferer he could not get better, but prepare for the worst. Dr. Constable, St. George's Road, said he was in an advanced stage of consumption. The poor sufferer was treated by each for some time. The man stated that at the different hospitals the doctors gave and recommended tobacco, malt, and spirituous liquors (I can prove that alcoholic drinks and tobacco weaken the nerves, heart, and digestion, which will cause consumption, and increase inflammation and ulceration in disease.) The poor man raised about a pint of phlegm in twelve hours, also at times large quantities of blood. He improved on the first bottle of my medicine; he felt better, stronger, and his appetite good, and he daily became stronger, was able to eat, drink, sleep, walk and talk, and gained seven pounds of flesh in twelve days ; and after four weeks treatment was able and well enough to go to his trade as a surgical instrument maker.

Who were the Quack Doctors in this case?

A few words to show the unreasonable foolish treatment this man and others received in the different Hospitals. Those with inflammation on the lungs, and consumptive patients, have often to lay with bags of ice on the chest, which must make the disease worse, as there is no possibility of this cold remedy dispersing the congealed blood, which is always in the lungs when inflamed, and causes such pain. Common sense shows me that cold congeals and contracts, heat expands and disperses. Working on this principle, by creating great heat in the system I cause a circulation of blood through the obstructed part. The above-named sufferer (Mr. Wood) said that he had morphia injected into his veins, and it caused him to feel like a drunken man. In Victoria Park Hospital and St. Thomas's Hospital he had flannels saturated with turpentine all over his chest, stomach, and back, which he said was horrible treatment, for it took nearly all the skin off his back and chest, so that he was not able to lie down for two days and two nights. I completed this wonderful cure with herb medicines without any outward application or pain.

A wonderful cure of Liver Disease in 12 days

After two doctors gave the man up to die. Mr. Turner, residing in North Street, Kennington Road, was visited by two doctors four times a day. On Friday evening they said there was no hope of his recovery, they gave the man, who was too weak to sit up or speak, strong mercury medicine that purged him violently from the Friday evening until Sunday afternoon. I was sent for, and found the man lying like a corpse, with his mouth open, and insensible, with no power to move or speak. My medicine was given to him, which he said the next day, when he could speak a little, he knew nothing about, nor did he know the medicine had been given him. With God's remedies which He sent to cure disease, and His blessing, this man was able to go to his work as coachman in 12 days.

Consumption Cured.—

Mr. Kent, jun., of 3, Lime Tree Walk, Sevenoaks, was cured by me of inflammation and ulcerated lungs, and a bad cough. He is now strong and in good health.

Bad case of Eczema cured.—

A Lady in the London Road, Sevenoaks, was cured by me of the above dreadful disease, after Dr. Don and a doctor in London had failed to do her any good.

Chronic Bronchitis cured in three months.—

Mr. Fredericks, of Quaker's Hall, St. John's, Sevenoaks, had been ill 12 years, and given up by the doctors as incurable. He had a bad cough, much phlegm on his chest, and his breath so bad, that at times he could not lie down in bed. Through taking my harmless herbal medicine he is now able to do a good day's work, and the last three winters has been able to work out of doors and in his garden. His son I have so far cured of consumption (after the doctors had given him up) with my medicine that he can take up a sack of potatoes from the ground and carry it.

Consumption Cured.—

A young woman in Ipswich was cured by me after two doctors had given her up to die. Names of doctors and the patient can be given.

Chronic Liver Disease and Debility Cured.—

Mr. Canney, St. George's Road, Camberwell, had not been able to work for two years and a half; in ten days after taking my medicine he was able to do a good day's work.

Croup, Bronchitis, and Whooping Cough in children cured in a few days, after being given up to die.

Paralysis Cured in three months.—

Captain Moffatt, of Mill Hill, Isle of Wight, was paralysed on one side, his arm fixed down to his side he was not able to lift it up. I cured this gentleman, although he was over 70 years of age, in three months, so that he could hold a chair out at arm's length (with the arm that had been paralysed) for several minutes.

Who are the Quacks?

Those who rob the public of their money and their life, through not understanding their business, and not knowing the use of the herbs our wise Creator sent for the use of man.

Cure of Consumption.—

After army doctors had failed, I cured Mr. Pettit, now of 48, Bramford Road, Ipswich (lately a non-commissioned officer.) I also cured his wife of Erysipelas and his child of Croup.

Cure of Croup and Bronchitis.—

I cured a child of Mrs. Harris, 35, Sidney Square, Glengall Road, Peckham, London, after a doctor from Peckham Park Road Dispensary had given up the case as hopeless.

Who was the Quack in this case?

Cure of Croup.—

After doctors failed, I cured a child of Mr. Pitt, 24, Friar Street, Blackfriars Road, London, by bringing away from the windpipe two pieces of congealed phlegm, nearly as large as one's little finger, and long and hard, like the roe of a fish. The child has enjoyed good health ever since (over five years). I also cured Mrs. Pitt of a frightfully bad leg ; and a daughter of the same family who was burnt to the bones in her arms, body, and face, and the doctors had said there was no hope of her recovery.

Who are the Quacks?

Wonderful Cure of Inflammation on the Lungs, and a Fever.—

Mrs. Preston, of Lyham Road, Cornwall Road, Brixton, had been ill some months, and treated by five doctors. Though they were expecting her death when I commenced to treat her, on the fourth day after she was able to attend to business as a greengrocer. For this cold and inflammation which had caused a burning fever and delirium, the doctors had been using (with lowering poisonous medicines) ice on her chest; but for what purpose? To freeze the blood in the veins and cause the disease to remain there. This is what it does. The faculty forget that cold is an enemy to life; to be cold is to be dead, and warmth is life. We ought not to have to teach this lesson in the nineteenth century. On the other hand, if the faculty know this, why do they still persist in using the direct agents to take away that heat, and consequently life? Heat is to life and health what steam is to the engine—the grand propelling power. As an engine requires heat to force the steam through the pipes to work that engine, so that wonderful engine, the human body, requires heat to circulate the blood through the veins to remove obstructions caused by cold, &c. My object in thus explaining this in so simple and direct a manner, is to convince the public that the medical profession wants reforming, and to this great and grand purpose I and many others, such as Coffin, Beach, Thomson, and all those illustrious men of the past have devoted nearly the whole of their lives to the study of botanic medicines, so that those stricken with disease may be able to get effectual and permanent cure.

I have shown how the mass of doctors, past and present, contradict each other. Who can put any faith in the practice they embrace? I have shown how unsuccessful they are in the treatment of disease, and how, by the blessing of God I have been able to raise up poor suffering creatures after the doctors and hospitals have given them up as incurable.

Consumption of the Bowels Cured.—

The child of Mr. Stafford, 11, Aslam Place, Sumner Road, Peckham, S.E., when 15 months old was taken to Guy's Hospital, suffering from consumption of the bowels (*Tabes mesenterica*); and after being under treatment some time was pronounced incurable. Dr. Webb prescribed for the child, but gave no hopes ; the child was then two years old. Dr. Howell, of Peckham, would not undertake to prepare medicine for the child, as he said it was a hopeless case. Dr. Bloomfield was called to see the child ; he took a small bottle from his pocket, broke the head off a match, fastened a piece of wadding on the stick, and dipped it in the bottle, which contained some *powerful irritant poison*, and traced it all over the child's back : this raised a lot of blisters in a few minutes, and made the back very bad. In a few days he ordered a large blister to be put on the back, when the previous sores had not healed ; this made it in a most dreadful condition. (What inhuman treatment, to punish the poor child like this ! Many doctors think that blistering on the outside will kill the inward disease, but this is a mistaken idea.) The child was then taken to Brighton and put under the care of a doctor, but, getting no relief, it was taken to another doctor, who also did no good. It was then taken to Dr. Edmonds, sen., Southampton Street, Camberwell, who gave it some medicine ; after doctoring it some time he gave no hope of it living, and said the child was suffering from windy dropsy, enlargement of the brain, and consumption of the bowels. As a last resource, the child (in a dying state) was brought to my house ; I gave the mother a bottle of my harmless herbal medicine, with directions how to use it, In four days the mother called again, and the little fellow was running by her side : she took another bottle of medicine for the child, and he has not been laid up since—over three years.

Who was the Quack?

Cure of Syphilis.—

A gentleman in Cork Street, Camberwell, was a patient in Middlesex Hospital, under Dr. Harley, for two months without benefit: he was a patient in University Hospital under Sir H. Thompson for three months ; and left both these hospitals as incurable, with a discharge from the great toe which was very bad. He had one bottle of my medicine, and a week after he came to me and declared, in the presence of a doctor and other witnesses, that he was cured ; he thanked me for curing him, and said he would call and tell his former doctors how he was cured.

Who was the Quack?

Cure of a very Bad Leg.—

Mrs. Bird, Waterloo Place, Camberwell, cured afte
several doctors could do her no good ; she was unable t
stand, and fainted every time her leg was dressed by th
doctors.

A wonderful Cure of Injured Hip.—

Miss Carden, 53, Brunswick Street, Stamford Stree
London, S.E., fell from a chair, seriously injuring her hi
and thigh, and being very much bruised; a fortnight afte
the fall she was unable to put her foot to the ground, an
was very ill in herself. She was taken to St. Thomas
Hospital, and there seen by several doctors, who pr
nounced the case very serious—in fact, they said sh
would never walk again ; she continued to get worse f
16 weeks, and her leg became withered. She was als
seen by two doctors in the neighbourhood of Stamfor
Street, who also said she would be a cripple for life. Sh
then became seriously ill, and applied to me for herb
treatment ; in a very short time after taking my medicin
she could walk without crutches, has enjoyed good heal
ever since, and is able to walk daily to her business in th
City. Over twenty doctors had told her she would nev
walk again.

Who were the Quacks?

Cure of Diarrhœa.—

A child of Mr. Crabb's, 17,White Lion Street, Bishop
gate, E.C., was suffering from protracted diarrhœa.
was given up at Guy's Hospital, as they could do r
more for the child, it had convulsive fits which general
precede death in cases of diarrhœa. I gave th
father a penny packet of Meadow Sweet, or Quee
of the Meadow, to make tea for the child ; the first do
checked the complaint, in a week the child was in h
usual health, and a colour in his cheeks. He had r
more medicine than this pennyworth of herbs.

Who was the Quack?

Through the extortion of some (especially lady) herbalists, many poor sufferers are afraid to come to me for medicine which would save their lives. I use the essences, extracts, pure juices, and the active principles of the harmless herbs, which cost a hundred times more than mineral medicines. My terms are *not* one guinea for taking away a tapeworm, but 3s. or 4s.; not a guinea or two down for the first bottle and advice, and five or six guineas for so many weeks' treatment, but a large bottle of good medicine, and pills, for 2s. 6d., in some cases a little less, or a trifle more.

So come, poor sufferer, and have a cheap medicine, and refuse the deadly mineral poisons which you might get from allopathic or homœopathic doctors, or at the cheap dispensaries for 1s. a week when ill. This supposed cheap treatment is very dear, for it costs the doctors' victim his money and life.

All kinds of Disease successfully treated

BY

W. D. STOKES,

35, Calverley Road, Tunbridge Wells, Kent.

He has not only cured the cases before-mentioned, but thousands of others, and he will undertake to cure or benefit the most hopeless cases. If he fails to do what he promises, namely, restore to health or benefit patients, **he will forfeit all his medicine and attendance, and will charge nothing.**

Letters detailing symptoms, or naming the disease, will have immediate attention.

Herbs, Pills, or Medicines, for all kinds of complaints, sent to all parts of the civilized world.

The names of the doctors who failed to cure the cases named, cannot fail to convince the most prejudiced, as reason will show it would be a libel to use doctors' names if my statements were incorrect. If anyone can prove I have not cured the foregoing cases, I will forfeit £100.

Anyone desiring a supply of valuable information on the effects of vaccination, and other medical questions of great importance, should read a book I have written (after 30 years experience), entitled **"Truth v. Error,"** or the fallacies of the faculty exposed. It shows how to prevent and cure disease. Price 1/-, post free.

Let the Government repeal the Compulsory Vaccination Act, and pass a prohibitory Act to put a stop to this filthy disease-creating practice of vaccination, and it would save the lives of 50,000 people in England every year. Let the doctors and people use proper medicines, and all small-pox cases may be cured.

Cheap Books sold at above address, showing how to cure and prevent disease.

£100 shall be paid by W. D. STOKES, 35, Calverley Road, Tunbridge Wells, to anyone who can prove that during 30 years practice he has had ONE patient die of small pox, or any other disease, where he has treated the case from the first.